Sophia the Spoon

Karla Neufeld

In the Land of Metal Things, there was a spoon named Sophia who believed she should have been a ring.

When those in the land
would pass by Sophia,
they would see her twisting
herself up or hitting her
scoop on hard stone walls.
Sophia was determined to be
the beautiful ring she
thought she should have been.
Day after day, the metal
utensils continued to watch
her try to change her shape,
but to no avail; she could
not change from the
sturdy spoon that she was.

One day, Sophia heard of a land far away
that had a sorcerer in it who used something called
fire to change metal things. She heard that those who
wanted to could be heated in the fire to such a
temperature that even the sturdiest metal
could be changed. By the hand of the
sorcerer, Sophia could become
what she desired: a ring.

After some thought, Sophia decided she would journey to find the far away land and the sorcerer who used fire. Bringing only her dream to be a ring, she set off on her journey.

When she got closer to the land far away, Sophia began to see metal items glittering in the light along the path – earrings, necklaces, and even rings that were almost lost in the dirt that covered them. Lifeless along the path were pieces of metal barely recognizable. They were dull, rusted, and tarnished from lack of use. Sophia continued on, but she was very confused by what she was seeing.

"I want to be a piece of jewelry like these metal items beside me on this path, but why are they here, rusting in the dirt?"
She questioned out loud to herself.

Deep in thought about this, Sophia didn't notice
a lone earring stud sticking up on the path.
She ran right into it and fell over. As she lay where
she fell, she noticed that the stud began
to move. Sophia's fall had dislodged
the stud from the dirt.

"Who are you?" Sophia asked the stud.

Coughing through a mouthful of dirt, the stud answered in a raspy voice, "I am Pertrude alone. I have lost my match. Who are you? And where are you going?"

"To find the sorcerer so that I can become a ring," Sophia said, almost jumping off the ground.

As she spoke Pertrude gasped and started to shake his studly head. "No, No, No!" he said, "You do not want to do that! I used to be a spoon just like you and now look at me." Sophia wanted to know more, but before she could voice a question, Pertrude was already explaining what happens when the sorcerer does his work.

"The fire is excruciatingly hot; the only way to enter it is to be completely dissatisfied with yourself." He said. "When I became that piece of jewelry that I had so desired to become, surprisingly, I was still not satisfied."

"I was lucky. I was bought and then worn for a time. Only rare pieces get worn for years and years. Then, after a while, I was thrown away because I was not in style and didn't look as good as I once did. That is why you see me and so many like me in the dirt now." Sophia was starting to understand.

"As the spoon you are, you will be useful for years and years to come. You have purpose and meaning in who you are. Don't make the same mistake that we all made…" said Pertrude.

"What do you mean by mistake?" Sophia asked quizzically, still not quite understanding what Pertrude was saying.

Pertrude paused a moment as he looked off into the distance and then said something that would change Sophia forever. "Love who you are created to be, and you will enjoy life in greater fullness than anything you can imagine at this moment." As he said this, it was as if all the pieces and parts of jewelry that were in the dirt with him rose up to echo their agreement.

There was something so moving in that moment
that Sophia's dream began to change.
She pictured herself as the ring she always
desired to be, but this time, she was
tarnished, thrown amongst those beside
her in the dirt, forgotten and discarded. Now,
she did not like the feeling that came with
picturing herself as something different
than the spoon that she was.

Sophia decided to work on loving who she was, the way she was, rather than trying to live life to change into something she was not. After thanking Pertrude, Sophia started the journey home.

Now able to embrace her spoon features, Sophia joyfully wrapped around her beautiful handle an orange ribbon that she found on her journey home. She marched back into the Land of Metal Things walking straighter and more confident than she had ever walked before. She no longer wished she was something else. She was proud of what she was created to be, a sturdy spoon.

Sophia the Spoon
Text and illustrations
Copyright © 2015
by Karla Neufeld
All rights reserved,
including the right
of reproduction in whole
or in part in any form.

First Edition

Watercolor paints
and a black pen
were used for the
full-color art.
The text type is
Tempus Sans ITC.

ISBN-10: 1515281361
ISBN-13: 978-1515281368

Made in the USA
Charleston, SC
26 September 2015